DEMARCU
and the Solar Calendar

Written by Quineka Ragsdale
Illustrated by: Darryl D.

FOR THOSE IN SEARCH OF KNOWLEDGE OF SELF

CHAPTER 1
THE EARTH STOPPED SPINNING

I'm not sure how I get myself into these situations. Joey and I were simply talking about college football and somehow Dejon entered the conversation. I knew something bad would happen because Dejon didn't have the best attitude, and Joey walked around like he owned the world.

Lunch was over and Joey and I were hanging out in our usual spot, at the picnic tables by the basketball court. We hardly get the opportunity to play basketball after lunch, because the older guys take privilege. I guess the new kid, Dejon, thought hanging around us was okay because I was one of the only students who didn't treat him like he was an ex-con.

Dejon was a cool kid, but he obviously came from a rough background. His face was turned into a permanent scowl. He walked with a funny limp. His clothes were designer labels but they swallowed his lean frame. Today he was wearing a huge, gold chain around his neck, just like the famous rappers. He towered the other sixth graders, and we heard rumors that he had flunked a grade. I think he flunked two, but he wouldn't disclose his age. The girls liked him because he already had muscles, but all of them were afraid to talk to him. I don't think he fit in with the older kids, either. I kind of felt sorry for him, so I didn't ignore him, but I definitely didn't go out of my way to speak to him.

Joey sat on top of the metal picnic table while Dejon and I stood to the left and right of him.

"Who got next?" I heard our star basketball player, Champ ask.

Just when I thought I had found an excuse to leave our college football conversation, Joey began to offer his usual charm. "What do you know about college football Dejon; you probably don't even have a TV." That was my cue to hang around a little bit longer. Dejon's permanent scowl was often followed by his short temper.

Dejon's nose started to flare. I didn't' know what that meant, but I was sure it couldn't have been anything good.

"What's that supposed to mean?" Dejon asked.

"Joey's always trying to be funny. Don't worry about it Dejon. I think we'd better head in. The bell is about to ring." As if on cue, the bell rang. Everyone, except the three of us, began walking inside.

"I'm not trying to be funny," Joey chimed in, "I heard that you were dirt poor and that your mom couldn't even afford to buy food. How do you have a TV?"

The earth stopped spinning. Dejon's only response was his fist's cock and release, all in one motion, that connected with the underside of Joey's jaw. In just a blink, Joey's body flipped over the picnic table and he landed on the concrete. I think I even saw birds chirping around Joey's head.

Dejon met Joey on the other side of the picnic table. He hovered over him, awaiting his next response. Joey had no words. As a matter of fact, I didn't think Joey was even inside of his own body. The lights were on, but no one was home.

All of the other students were already inside the school building, but a few began to gather around the window, staring straight at us. At least one of them had to have seen the whole thing.

I squeezed in front of Dejon, blocking him from Joey. "Leave him alone Dejon." I helped Joey up off the floor. It appeared that Joey was coming to himself.

3

"You got something else to say Joey?" Dejon's voice boomed like a grown up. I was even afraid of him in that moment.

"You really hurt him Dejon! Get away!" I hoped that I wasn't upsetting Dejon to where he'd want to hit me, but I didn't want him to hurt Joey anymore.

"Is there a problem gentleman?" A teacher yelled from the school's entrance.

"Get away Dejon, or I'll tell on you right now!" I said while still holding Joey's arm.

"No ma'am," Dejon called back as he ran toward the entrance.

"Get to class," she reminded us as she closed the door. Dejon slipped in.

Joey and I stood there alone, next to the picnic table.

"Joey, are you all right?"

"Ouch," he said. Joey held his jaw. He looked frantic as if he had just remembered what had happened. "Where's Dejon?"

"He's gone to class, which is where we need to go."

"I'm going to get that thug expelled from school."

4

CHAPTER 2
HE WAS ALL BARK AND NO BITE

Middle school was very different than elementary school. The teachers here didn't intrude on our privacy like they did in elementary. As a matter of fact, we were sometimes downright ignored. This is why I was able to use the history class I shared with Joey as a time to calm him down. The history teacher didn't interrupt us the entire time we talked.

I couldn't believe that Joey was actually mad at me for not attacking Dejon for him.

"You should be happy that I stopped Dejon from hitting you again."

"I'll have that thug kicked out of school forever. I'll have him put in jail. You know I can because my dad's a lawyer."

"You talked about his mom and said he was too poor to afford a TV. You have to understand that that is insulting." I pleaded with Joey. I'm sure somewhere within his pencil frame, there was some kind of empathy.

"Why are you sticking up for that bully? Is he your homeboy or something?"

"Look Joey, I guess I should have told you before that you can't stereotype people like that. We've been friends since kindergarten, so I don't care, but other people aren't so forgiving."

Joey and I were good friends, but he was so insensitive. He made fun of people's clothes, their accents, their race and anything else he could find that was different. Most people would ignore him, but if they at all seemed offended, he would even make fun of that. No one challenged him because he was as small as a fly. He was basically harmless. Like a Chihuahua, he was all bark and no bite, but I think he struck a nerve with Dejon.

"He hit me Demarcus!"

"You talked about his mom and then you insulted him. What did you expect?"

Joey looked hurt. No one had challenged him before and he didn't know what to do.

"Besides, I don't think many people saw it, but if you tell on him, everyone will know that you lost that fight and you'll never get respect from the big kids."

Slowly, he appeared to agree.

"Look, I'll talk to Dejon and make sure he stays away from you, just don't say anything else to him

6

anymore. If all those things you said about him were true, you probably hurt his feelings."

"Okay Demarcus, you keep him away from me and I won't tell. If he so much as looks at me again, I'll make sure he is in jail for sure."

"Okay." I said. Joey only agreed with me because he didn't want the whole school to know he was knocked out. That didn't look good on any middle schooler's resume.

I didn't see Dejon again until after school. He was on his way to catch his school bus. I didn't really want to approach him because the bus drivers only waited a few minutes before leaving, but I figured it was the safest time to talk. It was Friday, most people were in a good mood and there were a lot of other people around. Surely he wouldn't try to attack me in front of a crowd.

"Hey Dejon, can I talk to you for a second?"

"Leave me alone bro, unless you want me to knock you out like I did that little pipsqueak."

I sped up to get closer to him. "But that's what I want to talk to you about. We want to make amends."

Dejon stopped dead in his tracks. He turned around with that familiar scowl. I glanced at his stance and saw that his fists were balled.

"Whoa, Dejon." I put my hands up. "I'm not trying to start a fight. This is a friendly gesture I'm bringing here."

"Do I look like I want a friendly gesture?" His tone and his scowl grew deeper. I didn't know whether to stay or run.

Two buses pulled away from the curb. Dejon broke his piercing glare with me to look at them. I thought to myself, that this was my chance to run. I saw what he did to Joey and I didn't want any part of that.

"Aww man!" he yelled. One of those buses was his. He looked back at me, now inching toward me. I looked around. No one was close enough to intervene. I knew I should have left that picnic table when I had the chance. I wouldn't have this guy on my bad side right now.

"Uhm…I, I can help you get home," I stuttered. It kind of sounded like a squeal.

"I don't need your help." There wasn't much room between us now. I squared up to get ready for the attack.

CHAPTER 3
I WAS MAKING TOO MANY MISTAKES

"Demarcus! The bus is leaving!" One of my friends from the bus called. I was afraid to turn around. I didn't want Dejon to catch me off guard.

"Do you want to stand here, fight and get in trouble or do you want me to help you get home?" I asked.

His demeanor relaxed. The scowl lessened, his hands were no longer clenched and his body was no longer tensed. I stepped back out of his reach in case he tried to sneak-shot me.

"Just help me get home. It's the least you can do."

Whew, that was close.

"Come catch the bus with me. I can get my dad to take you home." Dejon followed me to my bus.

"Where do you think you're going young man?" The bus driver said to Dejon. Dejon looked at me.

"Mrs. Davis, he's going home with me."

"I'm not authorized to take any students who are not listed on my roster. Either you come alone or neither of you get on."

I couldn't leave Dejon alone, especially after I had just saved myself from a fight with him. I hated that I was such a nice guy.

"Thank you Mrs. Davis, we'll find another way home."

Dejon and I walked off the bus. Mrs. Davis drove off. All of the other buses left, too.

"Is your dad going to pick us up or something?"

"We'll have to ride the city bus. My dad isn't home for another hour." My mom had taught me how to ride the city bus home so that I would never feel stranded.

We walked to the bus stop right in front of the school. He claimed to not have the $1.25 bus fare, so I paid for us both.

The bus ride took all of 30 minutes, but it took less than half of that time to convince Dejon to leave Joey alone. His exact words were, "If that pipsqueak so much as look at me, expect him to disappear." Yea right... I thought to myself. I just looked away and enjoyed the remainder of the ride in silence.

My dad hadn't come in by the time we made it home. Seeing this opportunity, Dejon impolitely began an unescorted tour of my home.

"We can wait in the living room or we can wait in my room."

"No, I want to see your whole house," he said. He didn't make eye contact with me. He continued to look around and touch whatever he could. It was beginning to tick me off.

"Where do you live?" I asked.

He looked as if he didn't want to answer, but he remembered how he was getting home.

"I live in the projects."

"Which projects?"

"The ones we passed on the way here."

I was really ticked now. Why didn't he say that on the bus ride over? He could have gotten off at his own stop. I was feeling a lot braver now that we were in my territory and unthinkingly decided to pull a Joey.

"How can you live in the projects and wear a $1,000 outfit?"

To my surprise, he was unfazed. He continued looking at my family photos while he answered the question.

"I stole these Jordans and these True Religion jeans from my cousin. My uncle gave me this Gucci belt. He probably stole it, too. These real diamonds on my neck came from a crack head and I bought this shirt with the front money I got from Polo. He wants me to work for him, but I'm not sure yet."

I started feeling uncomfortable. I had just let a generational thief come home alone with me. I was making too many mistakes. I got lucky earlier, I wasn't sure how many more chances I had.

"Don't worry," Dejon laughed. I didn't realize he was now staring at me. "I've already checked you out. There's nothing here I want. I do want to see your room though. What games do you have?"

"Do you steal video games, too?" I couldn't help but ask.

"I wouldn't steal from you. Your dad has to take me home. I'd get caught too easily."

I didn't know if that was a good or bad thing, but I took him to my room anyway.

Dejon looked around just as he did in the other rooms. "Looks like you're the one who can't afford a TV."

"You didn't see that 60-inch TV in the living room and the 55-inch in the den?"

"Yea, but where's yours?"

"I don't have one. I watch those." I looked at the clock on my night stand. My dad should be home momentarily. He followed my gaze.

"What's this?" He asked, reaching for the Solar Calendar that sat inconspicuously behind the clock on my night stand.

"It's nothing," I shrugged. The last time I let someone learn about the magic of the Solar Calendar, I nearly lost it. If Dejon was manipulative enough to obtain an expensive outfit, down to the accessories, without a dime, there was no way I was letting him near my Solar Calendar.

He picked it up and began to inspect it. So much for that thought.

CHAPTER 4
THAT'S WHEN EVERYTHING CHANGED

"Put that down Dejon. It's a very delicate item."

Originally, I found the Solar Calendar in a box of my uncle's old junk that was left in my room. After inspecting it, in the same manner that Dejon was, I was able to unlock its magic and travel to historical places.

Before unlocking the Solar Calendar, I didn't know anything about Black people before forced human enslavement. I definitely didn't know that we were responsible for the civilized manner in which all humans live today.

After losing it, having it resurface, then almost stolen by my cousin Ashanti, I couldn't chance losing it again. I became protective of the Solar Calendar after spending my entire summer vacation trying to keep it from my cousin. Once she realized its power, she found clever ways to possess the calendar, but it seemed her cleverness was no match to this guy's.

"You look really scared. This must be something important. He tried removing the rock from the cloth, but it wouldn't move. He tried to move the arrow in the middle of the cloth, but it still didn't budge. He kept the calendar in his hand, but continued to look around my room.

"Aww, Demarcus, I see you got a little swag." Dejon was shocked to see the "By Any Means Necessary" poster of Malcolm X hanging on the wall by my closet.

"Oh, you like that poster?" I asked, hoping to divert his attention enough to get him to put down the Solar Calendar. He still held it delicately in his hands.

"Naw... not the poster, the gun. Who is this dude?"

"Man... you don't know Malcolm X?" I was almost in disbelief.

"Oh, yea I know him." He didn't sound convincing. I moved closer to Dejon. Well, closer to the Solar Calendar actually.

"He was a leader in the Nation of Islam. He said that we should fight oppression by any means necessary." I didn't want him to see me staring at the Solar Calendar since he sensed that I was a little uneasy. I kept looking at the poster with him, while planning to snatch the Solar Calendar away.

"He and his goons were carrying guns all through the streets of Oakland bussing on cops, right?"

I knew he was confusing Malcolm X as a Black Panther, but educating him was the last thing on my mind. As a matter of fact, I couldn't wait to get him out of my house so I would never have to say anything else to him again. He could stand to read a book or two.

"Yea, that's right," I lied. I was nervous, but I was ready to make my move. My heart was racing. I didn't know if this would be the first move of an all out war, but the Solar Calendar was worth the risk.

"I want to learn everything about this dude. I want to be bad like him." Dejon stopped staring at the poster and shockingly looked at his hands. "What do you know, it's moving."

I couldn't believe it. He moved the rock and the needle. I stood in shock. A bright light appeared. Dejon's eyes grew large. He was excited, or scared, or something. I was still in shock. Standing next to Dejon, I couldn't even move. The light remained and Dejon was amazed. I came to my senses and reached to grab the Solar Calendar. That's when everything changed.

The scene from the poster unfolded in front of our eyes. Malcolm X stopped gazing out of the window to walk toward us. He had the rifle still in his hand. He sat the rifle down on a cloth green chair before reaching us.

"Gentlemen, how may I help you?" he asked.

"Do you see this?" Dejon asked me. "Am I tripping? Did you drug me or something?"

I stood in silence. I had waited all this time, strategizing what, when and how I would use this calendar and it gets wasted... again. Disappointed wouldn't begin to explain how I felt at that moment.

"You said you wanted to learn everything about me Dejon. So, explain to me what it is I can tell you that I haven't already left for you in my autobiography and my memoirs?"

"What?" Dejon looked confused. He turned to look at me. Malcolm X turned to look at me. I was annoyed.

How dare the Solar Calendar decide to work with someone who didn't even know the difference between Malcolm X and the Black Panthers? How dare I hold the calendar secret all this time, only to have it begin to work with a drug-dealing thief? I just wanted us to get back to my room to somehow fix this. I'd just act like I didn't know what Dejon was talking about and ignore the whole thing.

"Demarcus, you have a responsibility," Malcolm X said to me.

Maybe, if I remained quiet, Malcolm X would ignore me, too.

"You're not going anywhere until the purpose is fulfilled," Malcolm X said. "I'll be over here reading these papers until you decide to fulfill your purpose." He walked away from us and into the small dining room. He sat at the wooden oval table in the end chair. He crossed his legs as he opened the newspaper and began to read as if we weren't in his presence. I forgot that he could read my mind.

I didn't know what Malcolm X was referring to when he said I had a purpose, but my goal was still to get back to my room, so I would go along with it until I got there.

I turned to look at Dejon. "Look, you were fascinated about Malcolm X because he had the rifle in the photo. He was protecting his home. Can you imagine living during the Civil Rights Movement, convincing people to join together to fight oppression and racism? Everyone was after him. Let's go see what he has to say."

"But-" Dejon started. I walked over to Malcolm X, not waiting for Dejon to follow.

"Sir, what did you mean by my purpose?" I asked Malcolm X.

"I think you already know the answer to that question Demarcus." He said that without looking away from the paper he was reading.

Dejon finally joined us by the table. "Malcolm X, my man." He said trying to sound cool. "I bet you scared some folks with a big gun like that?"

"That gun wasn't to scare people. I just needed to protect my family." He was still reading the paper.

"I feel you man. I'm about to get me a gun, too. I'm about to go into business with Polo, so I gotta protect my territory."

"Is that right?" Malcolm X asked, still not looking up from the paper. "And when did you acquire this territory?"

"One of Polo's other dealers got shot a few weeks ago, so that's the block I'll be working."

This caused him to put the paper down. "Excuse me young brother?" Malcolm X asked.

"I'm about to come up man by selling drugs on the corner."

I want to say I was surprised, but honestly I wasn't. I knew what Dejon was talking about when he bragged on his outfit. That was the moment I knew he needed to get out of my house.

"You got a death wish young man?"

"Naw, I got a family to feed. What I'm telling you for? I thought you were cool, but you just some nerd, like this flake right here."

I was the flake.

"Oh, I get it. You think you're cool right? When you find out that I don't agree, you want to start the sob story about feeding your family? Well I don't feel sorry for you. I was the coolest cat to ever walk in any city I visited. Was the slickest thief there was and dealt with the finest designer drugs. Let me show you," Malcolm X said, as he put down the paper and stood. He waved his hand and the scene changed.

CHAPTER 6
YOU ARE STILL OPPRESSED

Before us, we saw the interactions of a young Malcolm. Dressed in a Zoot suit, he was well respected everywhere he went. All the girls liked him, all the men wanted to be just like him. Dejon watched the scene like it was his favorite movie.

"This is better than *The Godfather*," Dejon laughed.

In the next second, the scene changed. Malcolm X was sitting in jail. Caged, like an animal. We watched guards push the inmates around for their amusement.

"Okay, I've seen enough." Dejon said.

"Oh. Don't you think jail is cool, too? No matter how hard you think you are, every inmate gets bullied by the guards," Malcolm X added. "Or would you prefer to see death. I bet that's even cooler to you."

"Naw man. I know that's not cool, but you gotta live it up while you can. That's all I'm trying to do. I think I can make it at least five years. One of my brothers made street life work for like seven years and the other made it like five, and I'm smarter than both of them."

"Who will you sell drugs to?" Malcolm X asked.

"You know...the loser users."

"Do you mean your neighbors and your family members? The people who look just like you? Then you're going to pass down this perfect plan to your younger siblings I bet."

"What makes you think I have younger siblings?" Dejon asked. I could tell he was getting uncomfortable.

"I think he gets the point." I jumped in.

"No, he doesn't." Malcolm X said. "And you are the reason why."

I still wasn't sure how this was all my fault, but I was more concerned with getting back to my room.

I continued. "Okay, Mr. Malcolm X. After everything that has happened, do you think the pro-violence movement was more effective than the non-violence movement?"

"All this pro-violence against non-violence talk. These are nothing but distractions. You should have one goal: to fight oppression against your people. The root of every problem against Africans here and abroad is oppression. Be it the crime rate, the death rate, self hate, living conditions, no matter what, the root is always oppression."

"But, some say that non-violence was more effective against oppression because now we can sit in the front of the bus," I added.

"Young men, this is a testament to how you are still oppressed. You have given someone else power when you seek their approval to use the rights that God gave you."

"You're right." I stated. That's one of the things I had always liked about Malcolm. He was fearless. "You always focused on liberating our people no matter what."

"I realized that no matter what our differences were in backgrounds, philosophy, religion or economics, we had a common problem and this is what we needed to focus on. Your oppressor has a cunning way of making you think destroying your neighborhood was all your idea." He directed his attention to Dejon.

"I'm not trying to destroy my neighborhood." Dejon must have felt guilty. "It was destroyed before I got there."

"Then why would you make it worse instead of making it better?"

"I'm only 13, you should be telling that to the older people around the neighborhood."

I knew Dejon was old, but geesh 13? He must have flunked twice.

"You're the big man who's taking care of his family right? I should be telling you."

"I'm the man of my house."

"No, you're 13. You may be the oldest male, but you are far from a man."

"You said by any means necessary right? Well the Civil Rights Movement is over and this is how we have to get it now."

"Didn't you see? What you think you are doing is nothing different than what happened then. I studied a lot to learn why we were in these conditions and I worked my entire life to change it. You want to tell me that you're dedicating your life to doing the opposite? You're supposed to progress, not go backwards. I'm only here to give you the information. It's up to you to do something with it."

"Is that what happened to you? Did someone give you the information? "Dejon asked.

"See for yourself."

Malcolm X waved his hand and disappeared along with the scene.

CHAPTER 7
FUEL TO FIRE

Seconds flew by. I grew more afraid with each one. We were not in my room. We were with a waiting crowd lined up along the street. No one was talking to us. Dejon looked confused. Oh my God, what if the calendar is broken?

I looked around the busy city streets in an attempt to get an idea of where we were and why. It must have been around the 1920's because those bulky metal cars with the skinny wheels were slowly driving down the center of the streets. There was a huge parade going on and every Black person from the city must have been there.

Leading the path of uniformed soldiers was none other than Mr. Liberation himself. The big, bold, Marcus Mosiah Garvey. I was no longer afraid. We were simply in another story with the calendar. Maybe everything was going to be okay.

"Wow!" Dejon exclaimed. He was amused by the parade. There were perfectly-lined rows of women wearing all white dresses with matching hats, followed by perfectly-lined rows of men wearing dark uniformed

26

jackets with brass buttons. The men also wore matching hats that reminded me of the navy.

I didn't understand why Dejon wasn't afraid of anything. It seemed like he had been on these adventures before. I had been through a lot of these trips, but I still got nervous. It seemed that the only thing that bothered him was personal questions.

"Hey young men, it appeared that you wanted more information than Mr. Little could give you."

"Who?" Dejon thought for a second. "Naw-" Garvey cut him off.

"I believe you meant to say, No sir. You address me correctly or do not address me at all."

"I'm sorry, no sir. When we asked Malcolm X about how he got his information, we ended up here. But with all these people, it looks like you're doing way better than what he had."

"You cannot put me and other leaders against each other like a sports game. We were not in competition with one another. Each of us did what we could independently or collectively to advance the race as a whole.

"It's hard to bring a group of people together to fight oppression, if they are not even convinced that they are oppressed. With his father, Malcolm witnessed the very things that you are witnessing now, the organization of our people. With this, I was able to spark a hidden spirit in Malcolm at a very young age.

"I first had to tell people that they were great. I had to first tell them that they were not their enemy. Malcolm picked up where I left off. He was able to immediately organize, but still teach those valuable lessons right away."

"I guess. I can understand that," Dejon said. "Excuse me for my ignorance, but I don't know much about you." I'm not sure who Dejon was becoming, his entire demeanor had changed. I guess he changed his tone because he didn't want to feel insulted as he had with Malcolm X.

"I hail from the great island of Jamaica. I came to the United States to organize the Africans here. They were like a sleeping spirit. I knew if I could ignite that spirit in the Africans here, that they would inspire the Africans all over the globe."

"How far did you succeed?" Dejon asked.

"I did well as long as I was here, but the American government infiltrated my organization, the United Negro

Improvement Association, with their spies. Their spies, who look just like you and I, did a great job of stirring confusion. They conjured a way to put me in jail, then kicked me out of the country. It is hard to add fuel to fire from afar. It's also hard to identify every potential threat before it happens."

"I can understand that," Dejon said.

"Sometimes we are called to do great things and we think that we are not ready, but it is not for us to choose. The calling comes from a higher power." He looked at Dejon, but somehow I felt like he was talking to me.

"Dejon, you are a brilliant mind. Please don't waste it. Malcolm and I have put in a lot of work for you and we need you to progress." He took something out of his pocket.

"I want you to have this and respect it Dejon." He kept the folded cloth sealed from his hands to Dejon's. "Remember young men, Know Thyself."

Marcus Garvey, the parade, the crowd and the streets all disappeared.

CHAPTER 8
IT WAS MORE THAN MAGIC

We were back in my room standing side by side. Dejon now had the folded cloth that Marcus Garvey gave him in one hand and the Solar Calendar in the other. He looked down at the Solar Calendar, then up at me. He looked down at the folded cloth, and then he looked up at me. I didn't say anything. I wanted him to speak first.

"Oh, there you are," my dad walked into my room. I turned to look at my dad.

"Hey Dad." I was happy to see him. My dad would make sure that no fight would ensue.

"Who's your friend?" Dad asked as he inspected Dejon.

"This is Dejon." I tapped him to let him know to speak.

"Hi sir," he said. "I missed my bus today so Demarcus offered to let me come with him. He promised that he'd get me a ride home."

"I'm sure we can help you with that Dejon. Come on I'll take you now." I knew that Dad had already sized up Dejon. He would have a million questions about him.

Dad stood in the door way waiting for us to lead him out. I reached for the Solar Calendar in Dejon's hand. He was reluctant to release it until he looked back at my dad. He held the folded cloth underneath his arm so that I would not take it, but I didn't care about the cloth. I only wanted the Solar Calendar.

Just as I suspected, on the way back home from dropping off Dejon, Dad wanted to know the details of the oversized-kid dressed in the over-priced clothes. Without going into a lot of specifics, I told him the bus story.

"I don't know Demarcus; he looks like he could be trouble."

"Well, I don't plan on hanging out with him. Today was just a coincidence."

"I'm not necessarily saying that you shouldn't hang out with him. You might actually be good for him. Maybe some of that new interest you've picked up lately could rub off on him."

Dad was talking about my new interest in learning world history as it related to the African Diaspora. Every chance I had, I studied more history. I was preparing for the next time I got the Solar Calendar to work.

The first time I used the calendar, I could tell that every person I met didn't think I was that smart, so I wanted to prove them wrong. By the second time I used the calendar with Ashanti, I was ready. I answered questions, posed questions and was very inquisitive. I planned to only improve.

"So, what were you guys doing with the Solar Calendar when I walked in?" Dad broke my thoughts.

"He was just checking it out."

"It looked to me like he was trying to take it. Is there something that I should know?"

I decided last summer it would probably be best if the parents didn't know about the magic of the Solar Calendar, but I think Dad was growing suspicious.

"Sometimes Dad, I think people just want what I have. I just like the Solar Calendar because it's my family heirloom. Where did you say that great-grandfather got it from?"

"Demarcus, I know you're just trying to change the subject, but I'm going to trust you enough to believe that you'll tell me more when you're ready."

Dad told me about his earliest memory of the Solar Calendar. He said he and his brother were just

32

looking through some of his granddad's things and they came across it. They tried to separate the rock from the cloth and his grandfather told them to be careful because it was magic.

"That was all he had to say to keep us interested in it. For years he would say, 'In order to unlock it, you must first know thyself'."

Oh my goodness. That's what everyone I met through the calendar would tell me. "What did he mean by that?"

"I'm not sure. He never went into detail regarding the history of the calendar itself. He just said that an elder gave it to him and told him that very same thing. I really don't think he meant anything by it. Looking back, I think he was just as confused as we were, but was too afraid to throw it away. I'm happy we still have it because now, you're all over that calendar. Do you really think it's magic?"

"It's cool to have something that some old man gave another old man, who got it from another old man, but I wouldn't stretch it to say magic."

Honestly, it was more than magic. It was an extremely weird magic. When I first found the calendar, I got the pieces to move, and then unknowingly got the magic to work. After all this time, I thought I was making the calendar work, but now it looked like the calendar was working me.

For months on end, I had tried to get the calendar to work and it wouldn't. Dejon made it work within minutes. That part made sense because I couldn't get the calendar to work over the summer until it was in Ashanti's hands. What didn't make sense was that the calendar would not take Dejon without me. One would think after a year, I would know how to use the calendar. One thing was for certain, I would figure it out with the new clues I had just got from Dad.

CHAPTER 9
BOX OF ROCKS

Monday morning came pretty quick. I had already made up in my mind that I would avoid seeing Dejon. It shouldn't have been that hard because we didn't share any of the same classes. I even skipped breakfast so as to not have an opportunity to run into him.

After more than half my day was gone, I became careless. I spent a few extra minutes to talk to friends in the hallway. I strolled the hallway to see last week's posted test grades. I had almost completely forgotten about Dejon. Right before fourth period, I stopped to use the restroom. As soon as I opened the door, guess who I saw?

"What's up Demarcus?" It was Dejon. He was standing at the sink washing his hands.

"Uhm... hey Dejon, what's up?" I wanted to make a U-turn, but it was obvious that he had seen me.

"I had been thinking about that little trip we went on all weekend and although I have no idea what happened, I'm pretty sure that you do."

"I don't know what you're talking about."

Dejon walked into my personal space. "I think you do and if you don't want no trouble, I think you'll start talking."

I couldn't believe this guy. Yea, he was big and had a few muscles. Sure he came from a different back ground and was likely a criminal thief, but there was no way I was giving him the satisfaction of thinking he could own the Solar Calendar.

"Dejon, get out of my face." I walked away from him and toward the stall. He grabbed my arm. I looked at my arm and then stared into his eyes. "Let me go."

"Whoa, Demarcus." He let my arm go. "I'm not trying to punk you, Bro. The whole thing was cool. I had never seen anything like that before. I want to know everything you know, about Mr. Malcolm, Mr. Garvey, and that dirty rock thing. Tell me everything.

"I'll tell you later. Right now I have to get to class." I completely changed my mind about using the bathroom and walked out. Dejon was right on my heels.

"That's fine Demarcus. I can come by your house later this evening."

"That won't be necessary Dejon. I'm sure I'll see you before then." I walked down the hallway to get to my class.

I should have known Dejon was smart enough to realize that I was trying to avoid him. Now, that he knew where I lived, there was no telling what lengths he'd go to get to the Solar Calendar. Good thing he didn't know that the calendar was in my pocket the whole time. Who knows what he would have tried.

I thought about it. I could have Dejon completely wrong. Maybe he actually did just want to know more about what happened. No... Who was I fooling? This guy was more cunning than Ashanti.

After school, I saw Dejon lingering before going toward his school bus. I quickly debated if I wanted to face him or dodge him once more. I didn't want any surprises, so I chose the former.

I walked toward him. "Hey Dejon," I called out. All of his attention was on some girl. The closer I got to them, the more I could tell that the girl was annoyed.

"I'm Zolie," she said to him.

"Zolie, I like that name. It sounds exotic, just like you look." I think he meant that as a compliment, but Zolie didn't seem at all flattered.

"Exotic?" she asked. "What's that supposed to mean? You think I'm from a jungle or something." She rolled her eyes.

"Naw baby, I think you're bad. You got that pretty caramel skin and that long wavy hair. I hear you speak several languages too. You're nothing like these local girls around here. You're Brazilian right?" Dejon moved closer to her in an attempt to reach for her hand. She snatched it away. I stayed behind him, out of sight.

"Don't touch me. For your information, I live right up the street and this little game you think you're spitting does not interest me at all."

"What are you mixed with sweetheart? Don't you speak Spanish or something?"

"First of all, it's Portuguese and secondly, I'm mixed with Black and Black."

"Yea right. You're not Black. That's Black." He pointed to an older girl who was only a few feet away. The girl heard him so she walked into their conversation.

"What's going on Zolie?" she asked.

"Nothing girl. This idiot here thinks Brazilian is a race. He wants to talk to me because I'm exotic." She imitated a quotation symbol with her hands to show that she was being sarcastic.

"Guess that means you're not my sister then," the girl said.

"This ain't your sister," Dejon said to the older girl in disbelief.

"Yes it is dummy. Same mom and dad."

"Then why is your skin so dark?" He asked her.

The older girl put her arm around Zolie and they both began to walk away. "Never, ever date a guy like that Zolie. He's obviously as dumb as a box of rocks."

Dejon yelled nasty words to the girls, but they both ignored him.

I walked closer to Dejon so that he could see me. "You can't get mad at that girl because she doesn't want to talk to you." I had to say something after hearing his disrespect. Dejon turned around to see who was talking to him. He realized it was me.

"You know that girl think she's Black? Won't even claim her own race and she called me dumb. And I know that other girl is not her sister."

I had already wasted enough time with Dejon. "I'll talk to you at lunch tomorrow. I have to go catch my bus." I turned to walk away.

"Are you going to leave without this?" Dejon asked. I turned back around to see what he was referring to. Safely secured in his hands was the Solar Calendar.

CHAPTER 10
THIS AIN'T NO MEMORY

"How'd you get that?"

"Took it right out of your pocket. I'm good huh?"

I stood there confused. "When?"

"Just now, while I was telling you about those dumb girls."

Before, I had simply passed judgment on Dejon as a thief, but now I was sure that he was a very skilled one. As bulky as the Solar Calendar was, I didn't even feel it move.

"Tell me how this thing works."

I tried to play it cool. "I need to catch my bus. Give it here and we can talk about it tomorrow."

"You are only willing to negotiate with me when I have it, so if that's the case, I think I should hold it until tomorrow."

I knew that I could not let that happen. I heard one of the guys from the bus call to me to hurry. I was getting nervous all over again.

"You're not leaving with this thing Demarcus. We can talk about it tomorrow, but I'm going to keep it today. What do you call it anyway?"

"It's a Solar Calendar."

"And what does it do?"

"Nothing. I just like having it okay."

"That's not true. You have to be carrying it to school for a reason."

He was right. I could not let the calendar out of my sight again. It seemed like every time I did, it would come up missing. I thought that keeping it on me was the safest place it could be, but I was soon learning that it was not.

"Did you hear those dumb girls talking about Brazilians not being a race? I wonder why she said that, especially if she should know better."

Dejon was still upset about those girls, but all I cared about was getting my calendar so that I could get on the bus. Dejon continued to ramble.

"Do you think there are Black people in Brazil?" He asked me.

I was starting to think that maybe Dejon needed friends. He was always trying to find a way to spark a conversation with me and he was very clever at keeping me hostage.

"I gotta go Dejon."

"No, Demarcus. I know you know. I want to know how in the heck those girls can be sisters, be from Brazil and be Black. I don't want to sound like an idiot tomorrow. I'm going to give them my two cents."

Surprisingly, the bright light escaped the Solar Calendar. I couldn't believe that this was happening again. Dejon looked around himself in awe of seeing that bright light once more. I began to leap toward Dejon to snatch it from his hands, but I remembered what happened last time. I wanted to wait a few moments to see what the calendar would do, but I didn't want to chance that Dejon would go on a journey without me. I leaped to take the calendar from Dejon, and suddenly, we were no longer in the school yard.

It was beautiful bright day, but instead of hearing the sounds of birds chirping, we heard gunshots. My heartbeat surpassed the speed of a Venom GT. My hands sweat bullets. My head started pounding. Even the hairs in my nose stood at attention. I knew more than anyone that the adventures taken within the Solar Calendar were not real, but that was almost impossible to believe with bullets flying toward my head.

There was a strong grip around my arm and I was pulled to a nearby tree. As I regained focus, I soon realized it was Dejon. He used the tree to give us cover from the flying bullets. He looked a bit uneasy, but wasn't nearly as afraid as I was. He calmly observed the scene. He turned to look at me.

"I don't see anyone coming from behind that building." He pointed about 100 feet away from us. "It looks like the guys with the big guns are moving in the opposite direction. I'm sure we can make a break for it in a few minutes."

"There's no need to run."

A lady appeared directly beside us. She startled me. I think she may have startled Dejon too, because he took a few steps back.

This lady was decades older than my mom, her skin tone was dark like mine and she was only a few inches taller than Dejon. Dressed in a light brown, droopy dress, she looked a bit rough around the edges, but she was very kind.

"What brings you two to Angola?" she asked. Her voice was firm.

Dejon stared at the lady, like he did not trust her. "What's Angola?" He asked.

"You're in West Africa, my dear."

"Are they going to shoot us?" he asked.

"No. This war has passed long time ago. This," she waved towards the war scene, "is but a memory."

"What? This ain't no memory, lady."

"Excuse me?" The lady gave Dejon a stern look.

"Ma'am. I meant to say ma'am."

The lady looked at me.

"I'm Demarcus and this is Dejon." I said as a pointed at Dejon. "What's your name?"

"I know who you are, but you would know me by Queen Nzingha."

Dejon interrupted, "So, you mean to tell me that I can just walk in the middle of those bullets and not get shot?"

"What brings you here Demarcus? What are you teaching Dejon?"

"He was curious about Brazilians and somehow we ended up here."

"Why do you think that is?" Queen Nzingha asked.

"I have no idea."

CHAPTER 11
LIKE A TIME MACHINE

Dejon left our side and walked into the war scene.

"You have a lot of work to do." Queen Nzingha said to me. She followed Dejon and I followed her.

"The Portuguese were a despicable crew. They came to our land looking for gold. At first, we were reluctant to trade, but those advanced weapons piqued our military's interest. Eventually, they grew greedy and wanted our prisoners of war. We let them have them. Then they wanted to take more and more of our land. That's where we drew the line."

"Is that why you are fighting?" I asked.

"Yes. Almost my entire life was spent fighting these people off of our land."

Dejon stopped walking to turn to the Queen. "How can you fight in a war? You're not a man."

"Not only did I fight in the war, but I led my troops."

"Did you kill people?"

"Of course. I had to."

"Then tell me about it. Or, can we watch it in this memory?"

"Killing is not a joyful experience. It is quite a disheartening one. But what was even more disheartening was seeing our leaders killed, our children stolen and our resources plundered. War is not just shooting people with guns in the middle of the street."

Dejon looked around us. "That's what it looks like to me."

"Come see this." Queen Nzingha walked down the street and we followed her into a building. There, she was sitting at a table, talking with two men."

"What is this?" Dejon asked. "I thought you were trying to kill them. Why talk with them when this is your chance?"

"These men are not from Portugal, they are Dutch."

"They look the same to me." Dejon said.

"I am negotiating with them to help us attack and fight off the Portuguese."

"They actually joined forces with you to kill their own people?"

"Those are not their people."

I understood what both Dejon and Queen Nzingha were saying, but neither of them understood each other. Queen Nzingha looked at me as if she was waiting for me to step in, so I spoke.

"Every country in Europe wanted to take from Africa and they were killing each other to do it. It was not until 1884 that the Europeans realized it would be an easier fight if they all joined together and decided which part of Africa they would rob and destroy separately."

"1884?" Dejon inquired. "Well, what year is this?"

"You call it 1642." Queen Nzingha said.

"I get it now. The Solar Calendar is like a time machine."

"Not quite," she replied.

"I still don't understand why you didn't just cut their heads off."

Queen Nzingha turned to walk outside of the building and we followed her into another scene.

"This is why you negotiate as much as you can."

The Angolans were in frenzy, running from the armed Portuguese soldiers. Some tried to stay and fight, but were shot instantly. Seeing their fate, others ran to hide out of sight. All didn't make it because they were shot from behind while in full stride. Their bodies were seemingly thrown to the dusty ground. The ones, who were caught, were chained and sent off into the horizon.

"These families were torn apart and shipped to some foreign land. They stole people from our town, neighboring towns, rival towns. They didn't care. We thought they wanted our minerals, but increasingly they wanted our people. Who does that? Who steals people?"

"Apparently the Portuguese does." I added.

"I had to grow up fast to learn the ways of war. When at war, you have to do some incredible things to win. Things that you would never do otherwise."

"Like kill people?" Dejon asked. I was beginning to think he was obsessed with death.

"Kill them, torture them, starve them, intimidate them, you name it. Every day there was a reminder. There was no peace. We won battles and lost battles. Either way, they just kept coming."

A group of chained men were being led down a long path. Some of their faces were bruised, some were bleeding and most of their clothing was torn. It looked like these men lost their battle.

"Follow them Demarcus. They will lead you where you want to go." I didn't want to go anywhere. I'm not sure what she was thinking.

"Follow them now. I have shared with you enough." Queen Nzigha turned to walk away.

"Wait, wait, Queen Nzingha! I have more questions." Dejon called after her. When she reached the side of the building, she disappeared.

CHAPTER 12
POUNDING THE PAVEMENT

"I'm not following them."

"Really? You're willing to jump in the middle of a gun battle, but you can't do this?"

"They look like slaves. I don't want to see anything about that old stuff. We're better off if we just forget it."

"What?" I had heard that people could be ignorant enough to think that not addressing an issue would make it go away, but I had never really witnessed it. "How much better are we by ignoring the very reason that we have problems today?"

"Seeing slavery is just shameful. I'd rather see people fight back."

"You feel ashamed because your ancestors were kidnapped, tricked, beaten and forced to another country to work for free?"

"I guess."

"Do you think that their descendants feel guilty that their wealth comes from slavery?"

"Uhmm... I don't know. I never really thought about it."

"I don't know where they're going, but if she thought it was something we needed to see, that you needed to see, we're going." I didn't wait for Dejon to say another word. I followed the chained men and I didn't look back.

Really? Did he just say that he was ashamed that his ancestors were enslaved? As if they walked away from their civilized lands, rich with natural resources and fully intact families and said, "I want to leave all of this so that I can be tortured and forced to build someone else's country for free."

Then he had the audacity to want to step in the middle of gunfire. Even if it was not real, why would anyone do that? I figured this guy wasn't very smart, but I was starting to think worse of him.

"I'm coming Demarcus. Wait up!" Dejon called, while running after me.

Instead of the long trek that it would have normally taken us to get to our destination, we seemingly walked into and out of a dreaded, dark slave dungeon. We then walked onto a huge, overcrowded, run-down ship full of chained captives from Angola. We followed right behind a young boy who seemed about our age.

53

"Oh my God Demarcus. That kid could be one of us," Dejon whispered to me.

I nodded somberly to show that I agreed. The kid was the same height and build as Dejon. He had a small scar on his face. He looked upset, but seemed to be pretty strong. I think the captives had an idea of the fate that awaited them.

As soon as I set foot on the ship, I felt an overwhelming sense of death sweep through the air. I'm sure the length of time we were on the ship was less than a minute, but that was 60 seconds too long. After each glance at our surroundings, Dejon would look down at his feet. We struggled between wanting to look and not wanting to see.

In the short time that we were on the ship, we saw the unimaginable. The captives lay side by side with no room to move. They weren't allowed to use the bathroom and had to go right where they lay --right next to each other. The smell was unbearable. Once a shipmate realized a captive had died from their unsafe conditions, they would just throw them overboard. One by one, they threw little kids, women and men out into the sea.

The shipmates laughed at how the sharks would follow the ship to devour the next victim flung overboard. Sometimes, there were people who managed to escape their chains. Those people either fought the ship mates until their death or they simply threw their own bodies overboard. There was less than one-third of the original captives still aboard by the time we arrived at the dock.

It was finally time to leave the ship. I knew from research that a journey such as this could take as long as six months. The captives struggled to walk because their legs were weak from minimal movement. Their energy was weak from sitting in darkness with little to no food. I had heard about the harsh treatment aboard slave ships, but it was always something that I couldn't even imagine. I couldn't stand another second of it.

We followed that same young kid with the scar off the ship. All captives were ushered into one big area to be hosed with water in an attempt to erase the stench that covered them.

As soon as we set foot on land, I knew who our narrator was because he was the only Black man in sight, cleanly shaven wearing a complete set of clothes.

"Well this seems odd", Dejon said as we walked towards the man.

"Hey guys. Long trip?"

"I'd say." Dejon said. "Who are you? What's going on? I can't take too much more of this."

"Too much more of what?" the man asked.

"The guns were cool, but that ship really freaked me out. I want to get off of whatever trip we're on."

"You're in Brazil. Is this not where you wanted to be?"

Dejon looked confused.

"It's beautiful right? Let me show you my home."

We walked with the man past the slave cleaning area to follow him through a forest. He told us that his name was Zumbi and that he was born right there in Brazil and his parents came off of the exact ship we were on.

"I saw my dad. Pretty weird to see him at such a young age and in those conditions, but I'm especially proud because although he went through the terror of that ship, he was never enslaved."

He explained that his parents had been forced there from Angola. He said that they had escaped to settle in the great community that he grew up in. He was captured from their town of Palmarés when he was only six years old and sent right to the same area where the other captured Angolans were.

"I was forced to work for a Portuguese priest. I was but a child, but I never forgot. I was diligent for nine years until I was finally able to escape to return to my home."

Suddenly, we heard a loud struggle behind us in the jungle. Frantic, Dejon and I looked around swiftly to find the cause of the ruckus.

There was a young Zumbi sprinting leaps and bounds ahead of his Portuguese assailants. In pursuit, a crowd chased him with weapons in tow. One assailant, without a weapon, was fast enough to catch up. He leaped toward him and they both tumbled to the ground. The assailant benefitted from the fall because he landed on top of Zumbi. He pulled his arm back attempting to land a huge blow to Zumbi's face. Zumbi must have seen it coming because he dodged the blow while at the same time reaching for a nearby stone. Before his assailant could recover from the pain of his fist pounding the pavement, using his entire body's force Zumbi swung his loaded palm to his enemy's temple. His body fell limp immediately. Zumbi wiggled his way from underneath the lifeless shell.

The brief tussle gave the crowd the ability to catch up. Luckily a massive woodsy area was up ahead to shield Zumbi from the showering bullets.

We moved along with the fleeing Zumbi. The Solar Calendar had a way of allowing us to move along with him without matching his pace.

Zumbi finally reached a mountainous area and leapt his way in the midst of it. By the time the assailants reached him, they had no idea where he had gone.

"It took me weeks to get back home, but I was so grateful to have finally made it safely, without the Portuguese on my trail. Let us move on to my city."

CHAPTER 13
YOU MUST FIGHT NOW

We reached a busy, well developed area that Zumbi called, Palmarés. He said the area was home to the mostly African race of people who had fled the terrorism of the Portuguese.

We saw the young Zumbi reach the people in Palmarés. His return was a huge deal. People flew out of their homes to greet him. One man was more excited than most. The man ran up to him and gave him an extremely long hug. He began to cry. When the man pulled away from the young Zumbi we recognized his face.

"Hey, that's the little boy with the scar. Well, I guess he's a grown man now." Dejon looked confused. "It has only been a few minutes. How much time has gone by?"

"This year is 1670. It's impossible to get you to understand an event if you do not see the different pieces that connect it all together," Zumbi responded.

"Oh...I get it now." Dejon looked like he was starting to understand. "I wanted to know something about Brazil and you're showing me all the pieces. That's actually pretty cool. So that guy that we followed to that ship became your dad?"

"Yes and my dad was a very skilled warrior from Angola. He fought his entire life and taught me how to do the same. Our warrior dance is now very popular here. They call it Capoeira."

"Isn't that a mixture of fight and dance?" I asked.

"We are so eloquent in our discipline that outsiders thought it was a dance. It's a methodical tactic of self defense."

Zumbi walked us through the town so that we could sense the culture. The city looked very well organized as many of the ancient cities I had seen.

"You would think, for a city built by former slaves that it wouldn't look so well put together. "It appeared that Dejon thought the same.

"Dejon, did you not see that the people who were forced here came from well established cities. These are the same doctors, lawyers, warriors, and builders that lived in the land of Africa. They did not lose their skills and identity because they were stolen and reduced to servitude."

"Yea, that makes sense." Dejon responded. "So, almost everyone here is Black?"

"Yes, even today. The people appear different due to the government's attempt to whiten the population by allowing only non Blacks to settle here."

"Yea, they did that in the United States too," I chimed in.

Zumbi added. "The racism in today's Brazil is so sophisticated that it has some of the Black people here claiming to be anything but Black, in an attempt to fit in with the ruling power."

"Not Zolie. She made sure that I knew that she was Black."

"Our culture was dismantled and the history of that was destroyed. The people who understand what has occurred hold onto their identity for dear life. If we don't, who will?"

"How do you know what is going on in Brazil now? Shouldn't you only know of your own memory? Kind of like what Queen Ninzgha said?"

"It is not I. The power comes from the calendar."

Why did he say that? I was trying to conceal any power that the calendar had from Dejon.

"Demarcus." Zumbi looked at me. "He must know."

"I must know what?"

"Dejon, I'll explain it to you later. We don't want to waste time."

We stood next to a group of kids playing. They were attempting to do the dance/fight thing that Zumbi discussed with Dejon.

Dejon's attention was captured by the girl who was watching over the kids. The girl looked a lot like Zolie.

"Are you telling me that this girl is Black?" Dejon asked Zumbi.

"Yes, she is."

"See, we like girls like that?"

"Why? Because you think she's not Black?"

It appeared that Dejon suddenly realized something. "Well, yeah."

"So you identify more with someone who looks like your oppressor, than the one fighting to keep you from being oppressed?"

"How come no one understands what I'm trying to say? That's not what I mean."

"Then what do you mean?"

"I don't want to talk about it anymore." Dejon looked offended.

"We don't have to." Zumbi said. "But I do want you to do a better job of seeing the whole picture instead of just the part that people want you to see. Many people are lost in Brazil today because they take the identity that is given to them instead of knowing their own."

"That's not just in Brazil Zumbi," I said.

"Most of the things that people love about Brazil were started by the Africans who were forced here, but this fact is hardly acknowledged. We started Samba, Capoeira, even the customs of Carnival. Do you know the difference between the Black people in areas such as Brazil, Puerto Rico, Dominican Republic, Cuba, Bahamas and the Americas?"

"The people who colonized the land?" I asked.

"No. Where the boat stopped. Africans were taken up and down this coast. We all had skills, culture, morals and values before the terrorism started and we have done everything in our power to keep them."

A swarm of soldiers jumped out of the bushes. The young girl ushered the children into a home and the warriors went into action. The young Zumbi, who now seemed to be a bit older, along with his father and the other men and women came together to drive out the invaders.

"We fought the Portuguese, we fought the Dutch, we fought any invader that tried to disrupt our land and force us into the deadly life of an enslaved person on the sugar plantation. They even insulted me by trying to negotiate with me to hand over my citizens for my own freedom."

Instead of allowing us to watch the battle that ensued, Zumbi continued to command our attention.

"The Portuguese captured, tortured and forced over five million Africans into slavery here and it didn't end officially until 1888. I am proud to say that I grew to lead my troops to victory many times before I was finally captured and murdered."

Dejon looked surprised to hear that.

"I do not regret it. A lot of those children grew to live a normal childhood because of the protection that I and these soldiers gave this city. You must fight now, not for yourself, but for the ones who come after you."

Zumbi looked at me. "It is your job to teach. With great power comes great responsibility." He glanced back at Dejon. "Know thyself." He tossed Dejon a small metal statue.

He caught it with his right hand. Dejon inspected it as the scene changed us back to the front of the school. I knew that I only had a split second, so I took my chance. I snatched the calendar from his left hand and ran to jump aboard the school bus. It took Dejon a moment to realize what had happened. He looked up then ran after me. By the time he had made it to my school bus, I was in my seat and the bus driver drove off. I waved at him from the bus window. He looked disappointed, but he didn't put up a fuss. He walked toward his own school bus and continued to inspect the object that Zumbi gave him.

I was ecstatic to have the calendar back, but that was short lived, because I now had a lot of things that I needed to figure out.

CHAPTER 14
UNWELCOMED GUEST

I was in deep thought for the rest of the evening. There were a lot of things going on with the calendar that I wasn't used to. These last two trips turned into four. Each narrator knew more about Dejon or me than I expected. They kept talking to me like they knew something that they thought I should have known. I just didn't get it.

More important than trying to figure out what was wrong with the calendar, I had to find a way to keep it from Dejon. I now knew that taking it to school wasn't the best idea. I still didn't know how he got it from my pocket without me knowing. Every time I underestimated that kid, he'd show me something else.

I was becoming more nervous. This was going to be a rocky road, with understanding the power of the Solar Calendar and trying to keep sneaky, vicious Dejon away from it. Especially, since I had to see him at school every day. I was sure after that last trip he had grown even more curious about the Solar Calendar and I did not want to explain.

I blew Dejon off all week at school. Every time he spotted me in the hallway or at lunch, I kept telling him that I had left the calendar at home. I also reiterated that I wasn't sure what was going on. One day he called my bluff.

"I looked those people up Demarcus and they were all real people. How is it possible that I met real people that I had never heard of before?"

"I don't know," I kept saying.

"How come they knew both of our names and they kept telling you to tell me things?"

"Dejon, I don't know what you're talking about." I got tired of lying.

"I see why you're all into history now. You go on some secret mission any chance you want with that raggedy, dirty towel of yours." Champ, the 12th grader walked by and happened to overhear Dejon.

"What are you guys talking about?" he asked.

"Nothing Champ," I said.

"We're talking about a secret that this guy has."

Champ continued to listen.

"What secret?" I asked Dejon. I knew how this would play out. The same way it had with Ashanti. He would try to tell everyone about the calendar. I would play dumb and everyone would think he was a lunatic. I just waited for him to put himself in that situation.

"Nothing man." Dejon walked past me to get to his class.

"That kid is a little weird," Champ said to me. "Demarcus, I've been meaning to tell you, I've seen you play ball before and I think you may have a little talent. Do you want to stay after school with us tomorrow to work out a little? Some of the players hang around to play a little pick-up game with some of the other students for our own light practice."

Wow, I didn't even know the basketball players knew my name. "Uhm... maybe. I'll have to ask my mom."

Champ laughed. "What? Oh yea, I forgot you have to check with mommy first. Well, let me know tomorrow morning." We left for our class.

Later that evening was going as planned. I made it home. I looked underneath my underwear in my drawer to confirm that the Solar Calendar was in its place. I finished my homework before my parents came home. Then I helped Mom cook asparagus and dinner rolls for dinner. Dad made it home just in time to eat. Everything was going as scheduled until we bowed our heads to say grace. The doorbell rang.

Dad looked at my mom and I confused. We both shrugged, indicating that we had no idea who it was. He left the table to answer the door. A few moments later he walked in with an unwelcomed guest, Dejon.

"Hey Demarcus, your friend said he came by to hang out with you. I told him he could stay for dinner. Is that all right?"

No, no, no. That is not all right. How dare this guy come to my home unannounced? I see that he was trying to up the ante.

"Yes, its fine Dad." Dejon smiled. Mom signaled for me to make Dejon a plate while she told him where to sit, which was right next to me.

"Dejon, I remember you from last week. Demarcus didn't tell me that you two were hanging out." Dad was so slick.

"We weren't really, but it just so happens that we have a few things in common." I heard Dejon say.

"Like what?"

"We both love history." Before, Dad was calling Dejon's bluff, but I could tell that this answer got him interested. Dad often thought it was weird that I had gained a sudden interest in history and research. I'm sure after checking out Dejon he was surprised even more. I sat Dejon's plate in front of him then took my seat.

"Let's say grace." I said in an attempt to redirect the subject. "Dejon, why don't you say it." I put him on the spot, but this time I failed.

Dejon went on and on thanking God for every little thing in his life. He even said a prayer for my family. I swear that grace lasted at least five minutes. I was pretty sure that my bread had gotten cold.

"Amen," he ended.

My parents began to eat. "Wow," Mom said. "You gave a lovely grace."

"I have a lot of things to be thankful for, so I like to use that time as an extended prayer."

Mom seemed pleased with his answer. I could now add deceiver to his list of unpleasant skills.

"Tell me more about this history interest."

"Well there's this object that, like Demarcus, I've grown particularly interested in."

Oh no. I had to stop him. Dad knew that something was up with the Solar Calendar and this guy was cunning enough to read his interest. He would surely use this as a ploy to get his hands on the Solar Calendar or force my dad to take it away from me. I didn't know which I was afraid of more. Dad knowing its powers and forbidding me from using it, or Dejon being able to connive his way into getting it. I chose the latter, so I took a page from Dejon's book.

"I told Dejon before that I would tell him more about Marcus Garvey, Malcolm X, Queen Nzingha and Zumba."

"Zumbi!" Dejon corrected me.

"Yes, Zumbi. I have yet to make good on my promise, which is probably why he dropped by unannounced. Is that right Dejon?"

Dejon took my cue, just as I thought he would. "Yes, that's right I hope you'll have time to show me after dinner."

Dad bought it, or he played along. "You two have one hour after you finish dinner. Tomorrow is a school night. Judging from your lack of transportation, I suspect I'll be taking you home again Dejon?"

"If you wouldn't mind? Sir."

"No problem."

CHAPTER 15
I PANICKED

We quickly finished eating and went straight to my room. Dad insisted that I keep the door open, which meant that I had to talk really low.

"Really Dejon?"

"You left me no choice Demarcus. We could be partners, but instead you want to treat me as an enemy."

"What on earth are you talking about?"

"It's not a secret anymore. You can act like you don't know what the Solar Calendar is or what it does, but I know you do and you need to start talking to me, before I start talking to someone else."

"Just tell me what you want so we can get this over with."

"I want the Solar Calendar."

"ANNNNT try again."

"I'm serious Demarcus." He looked at me angrily, but he didn't realize that he was again in my domain. I wasn't afraid of anything as long as my dad was near. I got into his face to show him that I wasn't afraid.

"I told you before and I will tell you again."

"Oh, you want to fight now because your dad is in the other room?"

"Whatever I have to do to protect what's mines."

Dejon walked away from me and sat on my bed. Either he wasn't down to fight or this was another one of his cons. "Look dude. Like I told you before, I don't want to fight you. I mean, I would fight you, but I don't think that would help."

I just looked at him.

"I really do want to know more about the Solar Calendar. I did do some research after those little memory things we saw."

I couldn't hide my surprised face.

"I know you think I'm just some dumb thug, but I'm a person, too."

I wanted to tell him that I didn't think that, but who was I kidding.

"Everyone we met has in one way or another told me that I was wrong about my thinking, but they also made it seem like you were supposed to teach me something and you haven't."

Dejon was right. In all of that thinking I had done over the last week, I didn't sum it up to that. Maybe this kid wasn't that dumb.

"Now I don't know what a lame, smart aleck, pipsqueak could teach me, but after the magic I'd seen with you, I'm willing to find out."

I overlooked his snide remarks. "Ok, I'll make a deal with you. Finish your research, then tell me everything about the people and places we've seen with the Solar Calendar, and then I'll be willing to try it with you again." Surely, Dejon wouldn't pick up a book.

Dejon thought about it for a second. "So you mean, if I can tell you everything about Marcus Garvey, Malcolm X, Queen Nzingha, Zumbi and Brazil, you'd be willing to go anywhere I want with the Solar Calendar?"

I was reluctant to answer because he was taking the bait a lot sooner than I'd thought. "Uhm... Yeah."

"That's easy."

Dejon went on and on nonstop about details of each person, place and event that had occurred. He told me about Malcolm's spiritual changes, about Garvey's back to Africa movement, about Zumbi's military ideals and about rumors that the Dutch planted against Queen

Nzingha. He included birth dates, death dates, war dates and everything. He made sure to tell me little facts that are not widely known about each of those people.

I was in awe. Dejon leaned back on my bed as if he knew that he had won. "Not the dumb thug you thought huh? So, when do we go?"

I was a little upset. I never thought about what would happen if my plan folded on me. I thought it would at least buy me enough time to come up with another plan. "Why do you want this so bad?"

He sat back up on the bed. Demarcus, I never cared about anything other than money before those memory things. I'm pretty sure I was tripping, but we actually met Malcolm X. Does that not excite you?"

"It does actually." I sat on the bed next to Dejon. "What doesn't excite me is that I shared that with you. You have no appreciation for history at all and you are selfish. All I kept thinking was all of the questions that I could have asked if you weren't there."

"That's cold Demarcus."

"Then you shouldn't have asked."

"I'll probably be dead or in jail by the time I reach Malcolm's age, so I don't have time to waste."

I thought he was trying to make me feel bad, but I could tell from his demeanor that he was serious. "Why would you be dead by 39?"

"My dad went to prison before I was born. My oldest brother was murdered five years ago. My other brother went to prison two years ago. It's just a family curse I guess."

"What about your mom?"

He told me that he and his two little sisters lived with their grandmother, his mom's mother. They didn't receive much government assistance because his grandmother didn't have their identification documents. He said his mom came by every now and then to ask his grandmother for money, but the last time he saw her was 10 months ago, when she dropped off his newborn baby sister. They never really knew if she was alive or not until she showed up. When she did show up, she'd hardly give them any attention.

His story bothered me. I could never imagine being born in a situation like that. I realized why my mother told me to be grateful for the little things. I sat in awe.

"It's not a big deal man. Life is just like that for some people. Of course you and your weird little friends wouldn't know. Now let's get back to this Solar Calendar."

I came out of my daze. "This is the last time Dejon and don't ask me about it anymore."

"All right, All right. Whatever. Let me use the bathroom first, because I'd hate to see what would happen if I had to go in one of those memory things."

I told Dejon where our bathroom was. I was happy that he had to go because that gave me time to slip out the Solar Calendar without him noticing. I glanced down the hallway to make sure he was actually going to the bathroom, and then I closed my door for a moment. I grabbed the calendar really quickly, and then opened my door as if it had never been closed.

Dejon emerged a few seconds later. He saw me holding the Solar Calendar. "All right, our hour is almost up, so we'd better get going. There's no telling how long this is going to take."

I started to tell him that time stood still when we used the calendar, but figured the less he knew the better. I really didn't even know if this would work. "So, what do you think you want to learn?"

"I thought about this on the way over here. If I'm going to learn anything, it needs to be how to better my position now. I suspect I can't really change anything in time, so I just want to gain knowledge on a lucrative empire, so that I will know how to capitalize on it."

Before I knew it, my face had morphed into disbelief. "What?"

"Just think about it Demarcus. I thought about a lot of products that sell really well right now, but I figured I would need to play it safe, so I settled on diamonds."

At least he didn't say drugs. I had no idea about the diamond industry, neither did I care about it, but so far with the Solar Calendar, all things pointed to Black history. Therefore, I figured, how much could it hurt?

"What about diamonds?" I questioned.

"I think if I can know how to make people want them and buy them, it will help me learn how to corner the market."

"Corner the market for what?" I really hoped he wasn't talking about drugs.

"I want to be a good business man that's all."

I kept the calendar in my hands to see if it would work, but nothing was happening. I panicked a little, but I think I did a good job not showing it.

"Ok." I handed the calendar to Dejon. "Turn the dial to about there." I pointed at a position on the rock, although I wasn't sure if it was correct. I didn't want him to know that I wasn't completely certain how the calendar worked. I also showed him which symbol to move the rock to, although I still had no idea what part of the year was best for diamonds.

I was upset because it was working. It didn't move for me, but it moved for Dejon. I didn't know what this meant, but I didn't have time to ponder because that bright light appeared to let me know that we were going to another place.

CHAPTER 16
BLOOD IS ON YOUR HAND

It was sickening. Men, women and children were crawling around the dirt ground with cans around their necks, searching for something. There were armed, foreign men lined behind them, with machine guns pointed at the hopeless people, watching their every move.

Dejon left my side and walked toward the kneeling people. I was afraid, but didn't want him to go alone, so I followed. "What are you doing Dejon?"

"I want to see what they are doing. This isn't real right?"

Once we stood next to one of the kneeling persons, we were able to see what they were collecting. Tiny pieces of shiny dirt. There must have been hundreds of people around the floor while only several dozens of foreign soldiers watched them.

Dejon turned to look at me. "What's going on?"

"They're being forced to pick diamonds from their own land for these greedy scoundrels." A man came to greet us. "You wanted to know about this exploitive, evil industry, did you not?"

"Who are you?" Yet again, Dejon looked offended.

"I'm Patrice Lumumba, former Prime Minister of the Congo."

"Is this where we are?" I asked Prime Minister Lumumba.

"No, this is in South Africa. I have plenty to show you regarding the information that you seek, but it appears that you do not have a lot of time."

I walked closer to Mr. Lumumba. "Why do you say that?" I asked.

"I guess you didn't prepare for this journey. Maybe-"

"Is this where diamonds come from?" Dejon interrupted us. He spoke to Mr. Lumumba, but he was still standing next to the man, staring at his canned necklace.

"Most real diamonds come from here and other areas in Africa. This is one of the brutal methods that have been used to get them to you."

"Who are those soldiers with the machine guns?"

"These are the English, but does it really matter which European country is stealing our resources and destroying our culture?"

"So, they're picking these diamonds from their own land and just giving them to the soldiers?" Dejon asked. "Then, they're the stupid ones."

"Really?" Lumumba asked.

A soldier began to yell at the man standing next to Dejon. The man took off his canned necklace and outstretched his arm toward the soldier. He only took three steps before he was gunned down in his tracks. All of the people that he was close to were gunned down too. If we were really there with the man, we would have been gunned down as well.

Dejon screamed. He looked at us, panting frantically. I was becoming afraid myself. "I thought this wasn't real." He yelled at us. He raised his right hand and pointed at it with his left. A spatter of blood was on his hand.

I rushed over the Dejon. "What happened?" I asked.

"The man..."he breathed uncontrollably, "The man was shot. His blood."

"What's going on?" I turned to Lumumba.

"He wanted to see what stupid was."

"How were you able to make that happen?"

"It's not me that did it. The calendar has a purpose and no one controls it as much as you."

"I don't have control of the calendar."

"We don't have time to discuss this. Read the instructions."

"What instructions?" I asked.

Lumumba turned to Dejon. "Every diamond that you adore has the blood of your people on it, just as that blood is on your hand. You want to run an empire such as this one. Murder millions of people, steal their resources and control the market that sells it. How much could you make from 100 percent profit?"

"That really doesn't work where I'm from. I'd go straight to jail." Dejon responded.

"That's the point Dejon. Whole communities are slaughtered if they think only one person tried to take a diamond and these diamonds don't even belong to them. They made an entire diamond company from stolen diamonds and you are killing yourselves for the same diamonds that your people were already killed over."

"Look, here in Sierra Leone. Fifteen billion dollars worth of diamonds were taken from this area alone, and these people are forced to live on 30 cents a day.

"And if you think that's it, think again. This has happened with coffee, chocolate and rubber."

With mention of every resource, the scene changed like pages in a book. I saw Africans being forced to harvest cotton, then being forced to harvest cocoa for chocolate, then rubber, then gold, and then diamonds. Scene after scene they were forced to extract their resources from the earth and then give them to the Europeans. It was cool the way our surroundings changed, but what we actually saw was horribly disturbing. Just when I thought I was able to digest an image, it changed.

"Here. Near my home, in the Congo, this atrocity occurred."

In the middle of a grassy area, there were several small houses, with roofs of straw. Each house was carefully stationed on the large dirt roads. Hundreds of Africans walked about, seemingly in a zombie state. Every one of their arms was severed. I couldn't believe what I saw. The entire community was mutilated. I suddenly felt sick.

"What happened?"

"That monster, King Leopold from Belgium destroyed millions of people. He nearly wiped out the majority of the country for his greed -- a greed that he's passed down through generations so that it still occurs today."

"All this for diamonds?" Dejon asked.

"This was for rubber, but same difference."

"Rubber? Why would someone destroy millions of lives for rubber?"

"What are your bicycle tires made from? How do your cars get around?"

"Oh my. I would have never thought. I mean diamonds are something that people want, but I guess rubber is something that they need."

"And your country helped finance this genocide and almost every genocide you see on this continent. Have you heard of coltan?"

"Uhm," Dejon thought for a moment, "No."

I hadn't heard of it either.

"It's a mineral found rampant in the Congo. My people are continuously being slaughtered for it, but I bet you haven't seen anything about this on your media channels."

85

"Why are more people being slaughtered for it?"

"It is used in almost every electronic device created. Your phones, televisions, computers, you name it. Another child is murdered with every use."

"Well, it's not my fault." Dejon protested. "You're looking at me like it was my idea."

"No, I'm just angry about the situation of my country. I don't blame you, but you are surely a participant without even knowing."

"So, what were you doing while all of this was happening?"

"I was not yet born when this started, but I will show you."

CHAPTER 17
THE EVIL EYE

Lumumba changed the scene yet again. I still felt sick. This was a little too much for me to witness. I could tell that Dejon was bothered too, but I think he wanted to know and see as much as he could. I felt the same way when I had first learned of the Solar Calendar.

I had since learned that looking at history up close was not as nice as it was in a book. As a matter of fact, the words in the book did not explain any of the massacres against Black people around the world. Usually if we were told of any Black person prior to slavery, they were supposedly poor and uncivilized.

I now knew that racism was more than a word and I was now aware of why most Europeans were depicted as rich. I was beginning to question whether I wanted to see these things. How many other kids have seen disaster, after massacre after destruction? I was no longer sure if this Solar Calendar was a good thing?

"What's going on here?" Dejon broke my thoughts.

"Shhh... you wanted to know of me. Now watch, you haven't much time."

We watched an important assembly. The men on stage all appeared to be official. The crowd watching was massive.

"The independence of the Congo is the result of the undertaking conceived by the genius of King Leopold II," boasted a skinny White man.

"Wait!" Dejon exclaimed. "Isn't that the man's name who destroyed those people's arms?"

"You are wise. Continue to listen," Mr. Lumumba explained.

The man finished his speech and a Black man with beady eyes and round glasses took the stage. He basically said the same things that the White man before him said. He talked about how they were happy to work toward independence with the help of the Belgians. He finally took his seat.

Another man came up, only to introduce Prime Minister Patrice Lumumba. Lumumba wasted no time to speak directly to the audience. Immediately the audience awoke from their slumber. They were no longer going with the flow, but showed a spiritual glow with every word he spoke.

"And finally, who can forget the volleys of gunfire in which so many of our brothers perished the cells where the authorities threw those who would not submit to a rule where justice meant oppression and exploitation."

Lumumba had to stop several times to allow the audience's excitement to settle. The stage was squeamish. After sharing confused glances to one another, they gave Lumumba the evil eye. It appeared that Lumumba was doing the exact opposite of the men on the stage.

"It looks like those guys on stage are not very fond of you," I said.

"You know," Lumumba turned away from the scene to look at me, "some say this speech is what caused many to put a price on my head."

"You were murdered?" Dejon asked. He stood confused. I think he finally understood that each person we spoke to was already dead.

"In the most horrid of ways. I won't make you watch them beat my body lifeless, engage an entire firing squad, then chop up my flesh in tiny little pieces. I can tell that you cannot stomach another scene such as that one."

"Did you know that you would be killed?" I asked. Dejon stood in a daze. It appeared that he was still in thought.

"Yes, I knew."

Still confused, Dejon asked, "Then why would you speak this way in front of them?"

"Because I am not a coward. Everyone in that room thought exactly what I said, but no one else was courageous enough to say it. This is why the crowd grew so excited. We had all seen our country robbed in front of our faces. Not one natural-born citizen could ever profit off of our own resources the way those greedy pigs had on stage. Then, they hand select our leadership and say that we are now free? They pay our new leaders to sit in a position, collect their blood money while they enforce the same exact policies. Does that sound like freedom to you?"

Realizing the pride in Lumumba's explanation and the matched spirit from the Lumumba we saw on stage I asked, "So basically, you sacrificed yourself?"

"They offered me money many times and I would never take it. Those scoundrels forced my people to live on pennies while robbing them blind and making billions. Do you think you could do it?" Lumumba looked at both of us. "Do you think you can turn your back on money and sacrifice your life for your people?"

I was about to say yes when Dejon interrupted me. "I don't know Lumumba. You said they chopped your body into pieces. If that's the case, I don't see how your speech helped."

"Oh, it helped plenty. Do you see those people out there?" He pointed to the crowd that remained excited once Lumumba left the stage. "Their spirits were dying. They had just about given up and began to accept their fate. The spirit is a most valuable thing. I awoke a spirit that would have otherwise lain dormant or worse, disappeared.

"Those same people, on stage with me, paid others to be my rivals. People, who had nothing against me, now wanted me dead so that they could feed their family. It is hard for me to hate my own people. They did not create this hate.

"People questioned my decisions and my moves, but think of how successful one can be when you have many powerful country leaders throwing money to have you murdered. None of them want to lose the profits that they gained from my land.

"These filthy animals even murdered innocent elephants for their resources. They were killing over 50,000 each year. There was no way, I would let someone like that come into my country and ask my people for support at the same time they were suffocating the life out of them. I wanted immediate liberation, not paper liberation and I was willing to die to get it."

"I want to ask you a question, but I don't want to offend you."

"You can't offend me Demarcus. I am here for you."

"Why? Why am I here? Why are you showing me this? Us this? I don't get it?"

"Read the rules Demarcus. Know Thyself."

He handed Dejon a dirty rock before he disappeared. Dejon was too busy examining the rock to notice that we were back in my room. I was bothered and exhausted.

I slid the Solar Calendar under my bedroom pillow. I immediately yelled for my dad to take Dejon home. He looked at me alarmed, but calmed when he saw my weary face. I was completely drained.

"All right, see you tomorrow man," he waved at me as he followed my dad to the car.

CHAPTER 18
HE'D DIE SOON

I woke up early the next morning still confused from the previous night. What rules was he talking about? Why did he say we didn't have much time? I felt like I had missed something.

I thought back to every adventure. I remembered them all. I remembered what everyone had told me. They were different people, during different eras. They all told me to Know Thyself. They all knew of the Solar Calendar and now it appeared that they all thought I had known of it too.

Where could I have gotten the rules from? I ran to my closet to search for the things that I had gathered from the adventures. Most of everything I kept, except what Ashanti kept and what Dejon kept. I didn't worry about those things then because I was too busy protecting the Solar Calendar from them.

I had finally found it. I kept my items within a shoe box mixed with some old toys. Because my parents had unlimited access to my room, I had to be creative and hide my things in plain sight.

I looked past the ring from King Hatshepsut, the coin from General Barca and reached for the book that Ashanti refused to keep. Maybe somewhere, tucked inside there were some rules. I flipped through the pages and there was nothing there. The old, pamphlet-sized book was written in another language. The curly words were written in backwards paragraphed blocks. It looked more like a story than a list of rules.

I tucked the book to the side and kept searching. There was also a rolled up piece of cloth that I had received from Manetho. I still wanted to go back to Manetho, I was almost sure that he didn't finish his story with me.

I was careful to open the scroll slowly because it was very aged. Once I opened it, I remembered why I had put it aside. It was written in hieroglyphics and there was no way I could read those. I started to move it to the side as well, but thought that I should inspect it further.

The hieroglyphs were written in a list form. Like steps or instructions to something. This had to have been the rules. But why would someone give me rules that I can't read?

"Demarcus, we're leaving in five minutes!" Mom yelled to me.

Oh snap. I had been up all this time, but I didn't get dressed. I put everything back in the box and put the box back in its place. I changed as quick as I could, but it proved not to be quick enough.

"Let's go now!" Mom yelled to me. I ran out the room to catch up to her and remembered that I had left the Solar Calendar underneath my pillow. Although I didn't have time to get it, I was afraid that one of my parents might go in my room while I was gone. I grabbed it really quick and tucked it in my backpack. I caught my mom just in time.

"You were about to walk to the bus stop by yourself," she said. Dang, I thought. She already had the car in reverse.

I brushed my hair after I had gotten on the school bus. One of my friends talked to me the whole way to school, but I was too busy trying to figure out how I would be able to read the rules in hieroglyphics. I wondered if I could take an online class or something. I decided that I'd skip breakfast and go to the media center as soon as I got to school.

I hopped off the bus to make a bee line to the media center, but was disappointed when I realized I had an awaiting guest.

"Man... that Lumumba was something wasn't he?" Dejon asked with this goofy grin on his face.

"Yea that was cool." I kept a brisk pace to get to the media center, but Dejon made sure to not let me get too far away.

"I just came to tell you that today is my last day. I'm leaving the school."

"What?" I stopped walking. "It's not even spring break."

"I'm not sticking around this place. Remember, I got a new job anyway."

"Selling drugs Dejon?"

"Shhh," he looked around to make sure no one could hear us. "Don't say it like that."

"Did you not learn anything from Malcolm X? From Garvey? From anyone?"

"They made a lot of sense, but come on man, really? I have a situation to deal with today. And besides, the school wants to put me in some special education class. People already look at me crazy at this school. What would I look like then?"

"That doesn't make sense. I mean, you're not the sharpest tool in the shed, but after hanging with you a while, I know you're not that slow."

"Doesn't matter now Demarcus, I'm sure I'll see you around." He started to walk off.

"Wait," I said.

After hanging with Dejon those last few days, I felt like I knew him a little better. Now that I knew a little bit about his background, I now knew why he thought selling drugs was his best option. I could understand why he didn't have many goals in life and why he thought he'd die soon. Maybe this is what Malcolm X and the others meant. I was somehow supposed to help Dejon understand that he could make better choices. Not sure why I was the one that was supposed to do that, but it still made sense.

"What?" Dejon asked.

"Why don't you play a game of basketball with me after school, since I probably won't see you again?" I needed time to think about what Dejon was saying. Maybe if we talked again later, I'd have my thoughts collected.

He thought about it. "I guess so. I'll be around most of the day anyway to say my goodbyes and wrap up my things."

I made it to the media center pretty early, but had to wait 20 minutes for the media specialist to show up. I didn't understand how they say we can use time before school to work on our projects and the person who opens the door was not even available.

"Good morning young man," the media specialist said to me when she made it to the door.

"Good morning."

She had no sense of urgency. She had me help her bring her bags into the center, while she took her time to turn on the lights. I was in despair when I saw that the computers weren't even powered up.

"You better get headed to class, the bell will ring soon."

I couldn't believe this. I waited all morning to get to the computer and now it was time for class.

"I really need to use the computer before I go."

"Maybe you can come back on lunch."

Oh no. I missed breakfast, but I definitely wasn't going to miss lunch as well.

"I really just need to know if there's a way that I can learn hieroglyphics online."

She finally made it to her desk. She had a confused look on her face as she took a life time to sit down. The bell rang.

"Hieroglyphics? For what purpose?"

I was growing impatient by the second. "I saw an old sentence somewhere I want to try to read it."

"I don't suspect that you will be able to learn it online, but maybe you can find some community classes or something."

"Okay thanks." I rushed out of the center before she could say anything else. All of the time I had spent pondering over Solar Calendar issues had led me nowhere. I would just have to finish my search after school.

CHAPTER 19
WE HEARD SIRENS

I shoved my lunch down my throat like it was my first meal of the week. I didn't wait for Joey or any of my bus friends like I normally did.

"Dang little man." It was Champ and his basketball friends walking by. "Are you trying to get up enough energy for our pick-up game after school?"

Pick-up game? What...? Oh, I remembered. "Uhm... yea, I'll be there."

"Cool, I won't be here next year and coach has left it up to me, as captain to find potential recruits for JV. I think you'll be a perfect addition." Champ and his friends left to find seats.

Wow! That made me feel really cool. Champ was the star of the whole basketball team and he wanted to show me some skills.

"Hey man. Did I hear him right?" Joey came to sit at the table with me. He saw that I was almost done with my food and looked upset. "You couldn't even wait?"

"Dude, I was starving. I didn't eat breakfast."

"Yea, okay," he responded. "I'll be right back." Joey left to get in line for his lunch.

The rest of the day went by fairly quickly. I had thought about what I could say to Dejon to make him stay in school. I know he really needed to make money, but like Malcolm X told him, he would end up dead or in jail.

This Solar Calendar thing was beginning to be too much for me. I still didn't understand how to work it properly. I finally got my hands on rules that I think I've had all along, but I have no way to read them. It had me hanging out with a guy who was way different than me. Well, maybe he wasn't that different from me. We'd probably be a lot similar had we grown up with the same circumstances.

I think I was just going to tell Dejon to think about it for a few more weeks. I wish I could have told him during lunch, but we didn't have the same lunch period and he and Joey still didn't get along.

I went straight to the basketball courts after school. This move with Champ would surely help my popularity. There were already a few guys playing on the court, so I just sat down at the picnic table. Neither Champ nor Dejon was anywhere in sight. I unzipped my backpack to pull out my homework, but that's when Dejon showed up.

"What's up Demarcus? I don't have much time to talk because I have to get to work."

"Work Dejon?"

"Just because you don't like it, don't mean it's not a job."

"Look, I thought about everything you said and what I was told with the Solar Calendar and I think you guys are right. There's something I'm supposed to show you or teach you, but there's no way for me to do that if you're not in school."

"I've seen enough with the Solar Calendar. It was cool. I still don't know how you work it, but none of that is going to change my current situation. And I sure as heck won't be in a class that treats me like I have a mental disability. I'll show everybody when they see how much I move up at work."

I still couldn't believe this guy was referring to selling drugs as a job, but I chose not to argue that point.

A few more basketball players showed up at the court. "Where's Champ?" They asked the guys who were already playing there.

"They went to the store to get some sports drinks because the vending machine was out. We can warm up for a few minutes until they're back."

"Looks like ya'll are about to get started." Dejon said. "I'm going to go ahead and leave. Maybe I'll stop by your house next week or something."

"What if we used the Solar Calendar one more time? You have to see that this is not the answer."

"Demarcus, I know it's not the answer. I'm not slow. I just don't have any other choice. I've seen what my future holds and it's not like yours."

"They killed Champ! They killed Champ!" One of the basketball players ran toward us from the street. He was disheveled, sweaty and out of breath. Everyone's attention immediately turned to him.

"What? What happened?"

"The police pulled us over. They came to the car, got into an argument with Champ and just started shooting. I was in the passenger seat. He was still sitting in the car. I ran and didn't look back. They were shooting after me, too."

"What did you guys do? What happened?"

"I don't know! I don't know!"

I was in shock. The players were standing around the guy on the court trying to make sense of what he was saying.

I heard Dejon say, "We gotta go." He yanked me toward the back of the school building, but it was locked. We sat behind a wall close to the doors. I kept my eyes toward the scene.

We heard sirens. A sporty police car sped onto the basketball court. The boys had to jump out of the way to avoid getting hit. They dispersed as fast as they could. I had never been more afraid in my life. This was worse than experiencing war with the Solar Calendar.

"Make this thing work," Dejon said to me. I was still looking at the unbelievable scene. One policeman shot something to paralyze one of the running players.

"Demarcus! Focus!" Dejon forced my head to look away from the police officers and to look at him. I heard a gunshot.

He put something in my hands. "Why would they hurt them? Are they going to hurt us? What did we do? I should have gone home." I muttered over and over again questions that I couldn't understand.

After a few seconds, the players and the police officers disappeared. The wall that we were hiding behind was gone. Our feet were now planted on a gloomy slave plantation.

CHAPTER 20
HIS WHISPERING VOICE

"Gentlemen." A man walked toward us, dressed in jean overalls, wearing a straw hat. "Whoa, I'm feeling a lot of energy coming from you two." He slowed down to examine us.

"Yea man. We almost witnessed the cops kill some of our classmates. We had to get out of there." Dejon said.

I still stood in awe. I couldn't even think.

"I've witnessed those coppers kill a few myself. Looks like Demarcus is spooked. I reckon that's normal."

"He hasn't seen anything like that before. He's one of those people who think the cops actually need a reason to kill you."

I realized that they were talking about me like I wasn't there. I came to my senses. "Stop talking about me like I'm not here." I looked at Dejon. I didn't want the man to think that I was also talking about him.

"Oh, you're wake now? Let's start moving."

We walked through a row of crops lined with about 20 people working them. There were rows upon rows of crops and people, forming a huge grid.

"My name is Nat Turner." The man called as we followed him. "I work on this wretched land. All services for free of course."

Dejon looked around. "So, you're a slave?" He asked.

"No, I am a man—a man who was forced to work sun up to sun down for free. To merely call me a slave, is an insult. That is no one's destiny and cannot sum up anyone's life."

"I'm sorry," Dejon said.

Mr. Turner stopped walking to turn around to face us. "Look around you, do these people look happy?"

Everyone was busy working to pull the crops. They moved slowly as if to preserve energy that could last the rest of the day. A big man marched down the line looking at the men, women and children as he passed them. He stopped once he found the object of his search. A girl who appeared to be about my age was grabbed and thrown over his shoulder as he headed back the way he had came. She kicked and screamed, but was no match for the big man. The women that were around her began to cry.

The big man threw the girl into a broken down shack before locking the door from the outside.

"What did she do?" Dejon asked.

"She is being forced to lay down with men until she can produce viable offspring to help work this huge land for free."

"Oh my God, that is disgusting."

"You never get used to the daily torture and pain that happens here. You can either find ways to cope or you die."

The big man went down another aisle in search of another victim. This time he found a young boy --a boy much younger than me. Instead of taking him to the shack, he went into the big house. The boy and the people around him were just as upset as the girl and the ones around her.

"Do I dare ask?" Dejon asked.

"The one who controls this land prefers little boys."

Dejon gagged. I became upset.

"I don't know why, but this seems as bad as getting your arms chopped off."

"It's all bad. Getting stabbed in your right leg as oppose to your left doesn't make the pain any easier. But they say their supposed slaves were happy. How can one be happy when they can't even control their own bodies?"

"Is this what all slaves went through?" Dejon asked.

"You mean enslaved persons?" Mr. Turner said, correcting him. "You could get stabbed in the left foot or the right, either way you'd still get stabbed. Some of them were used as experiments, some used to kill each other for sport, and some used to simply work until their death. There was no such thing as a happy enslaved person."

"Who says they were happy though?" I asked.

"This is what the owners would put in the paper. They wanted the entire country to believe that we were happy to work for free and not have any control of our bodies. Come now."

By the time we finished our last few steps to the larger run down shack, the sky grew dark. Inside there was Mr. Turner standing at the front of the room. All others were seated around him, fully engaged in his every word. He held a bible in his hand and talked about loving the Lord.

"Who's the White guy?" Dejon asked Mr. Turner.

I didn't even realize there was a White man sitting in the back of the room, watching the entire scene.

"There could be no meetings amongst us without one of them present. They wanted to ensure that we only talked about a heaven after death, so that we would enjoy our hell on earth."

In the middle of Mr. Turner's presentation, the man in the back of the room stood. He told everyone to go to their quarters for sleep, for he had grown tired. Everyone started to leave. The man rushed past them to go back to his home. An enslaved man, stood at the door to make sure the man was leaving; he then nodded to Mr. Turner.

Mr. Turner's entire demeanor changed. The majority of the other men gathered around him to hear his whispering voice. He gave them instructions and they nodded in agreement before dispersing.

"We can't hear you," Dejon said.

I gave them orders that this would be the night to rid ourselves of this evil enslavement.

With an outside view, we were able to see Mr. Turner and his troops flee from home to home to murder all its inhabitants. They killed the men, women and children of their enslavers. They didn't want to leave anyone alive to return their families into the harsh realities of forced human bondage.

The killing spree was over when we saw the group of men, wearing copper badges, search frantically for Mr. Turner and his troops.

"Those badges look similar to the ones the cops wear now," Dejon observed.

"This is where your police system comes from. Filthy men, who were armed to seek out, torture and catch any escaped person fleeing from bondage.

"They harassed us continuously. Wanting to see our papers, know where we were going, why, and where we had come from."

"Didn't you think that they would eventually catch you?" Dejon asked.

"Do we allow our women and children to sit in fear for the days of their lives? No matter how much we were told otherwise, God gave us the same right as everyone else to walk freely in this world."

"So, how did this play out?"

"Those police officers caught me, jailed me, refused to give me a fair trial, hung me, and then cut my body into pieces so that they could pass the pieces amongst their friends."

"That's harsh. Maybe you should have kept working and not put up a fight," Dejon said.

"Or maybe they could have not enslaved us and tried to own the lives of other humans? Maybe they shouldn't have forced us to build this country with our bare hands while raping our daughters and sons for their own pleasure."

"What happened to the other people in your army?" I asked.

"They were murdered too. So were countless men, women and children who were all innocent. But you can't judge us for fighting in a war that we did not create. Only a fool sits docile while watching his culture robbed and killed in front of his eyes.

"It's still hard to believe there were police officers around who did not at least stop the rape and torture," I added.

"The coppers were trained for the sole purpose of keeping enslaved persons in line. Remember, according to

113

them we had no rights. Even after they considered us citizens, the coppers were still used to ensure that we did not advance. There was no such thing as coppers for Black people."

CHAPTER 21
JOIN THIS WAR

"When did this happen, because Lincoln eventually freed the slaves?" Mr. Turner glared at Dejon. "I mean the enslaved."

"This country cared about one thing: getting rich off the free labor of Blacks. Why do you think you're in the conditions that you are in now? They've convinced you that giving your people poison to slowly kill themselves is a good job."

Dejon looked ashamed.

"I killed those evil bandits in 1831 during the time they told the world that the so called slaves were happy. This Lincoln you're referring to was trying to keep this deplorable country together. We thought it best to allow them to rip each other apart. Do you really want to know about this Civil War?"

"I do," I added. I thought I knew about the Civil War, but I wanted to know what he knew.

"The northern side of the country was mad at the southern side of the country because they were making free money from the enslaved and were not paying enough taxes. They came up with the three-fifth compromise in 1787 to say that the enslaved could count as three-fifth of a person so that the southerners could be taxed more.

"This worked for a while. The two sides still didn't like much of each other because although there were less people in the southern states, they had more say over who could be voted into office because that compromise. This country swindled their way into California, the Louisiana Purchase and Texas. They constantly fought over who paid what taxes when they acquired states that were considered either northern or southern states."

"This sounds like a history lesson, but somehow it seems more interesting when you tell the story," Dejon said. I agreed.

"That's because when your teacher tells you the story, they leave out how it affected you.

"The southerners were sending their tobacco, sugar, cotton and other goods created for free from my very hands, off to English countries. The northerners kept raising the taxes on these southern exports. They didn't need free labor as much as the southerners did because most of their income came from their industrial businesses. The northerners wanted to get rid of slavery, not because it was wrong, but because they knew it would affect the southerner's power. The southerner was afraid that his position in Congress was dwindling with all the new rules imposed by the northerners.

"When Lincoln made the presidency, the southerners felt that they had no choice, but to go to war, because Lincoln would surely side with the northerners to cripple their economy and affect their position in the White House."

Mr. Turner showed us a new scene -- a scene outside of his timeframe. We were inside of a room with hardwood floors. The sofa and chairs had feet and there was a fireplace against one of the walls. Lincoln sat at a desk, while three men alternately sat and talked about the room.

"If I could save the Union without freeing any slaves, I would," Lincoln said.

"We have to end this bloody war and now. White men are dying by the thousands on each side."

"Send the negroes to fight."

"We can't give them arms. Do you want to affect the liberty of this good, God-fearing country?"

"Who would you rather see die in battle?"

The men looked about in silence as they pondered.

"The Union was doing a horrible job. They were losing this war and Black people on each side stood out the way to let them fight," Mr. Turner continued.

"I thought Black people fought in the Civil War too? That they even fought for the South."

"Let me guess. Your teacher forced that issue on you?" Mr. Turner said. "The enslaved persons that fought for the southerners were forced to do so. There was no group of Black people pleading to join this war. Not until Lincoln eventually changed his mind.

"He told them that they would help to end slavery. Black people were no fool, they ignored Lincoln's cry until he convinced Black leaders otherwise. He negotiated with the likes of Frederick Douglass and Harriet Tubman that this war was about freeing the enslaved. He also promised that they would receive free land in compensation for the brutality of slavery, so they finally agreed.

"Frederick Douglass printed this article," he passed a paper to us, seemingly out of thin air, "and Black men began to join the Union by the thousands. It became evident within six months of them joining, that this war was won."

"Wait, so Black people helped to win the Civil War?" I asked.

"The northerners were losing battles all over their own land until Frederick Douglass sent out that notice, but for some reason, someone wants you to feel insignificant."

"Maybe school would be more interesting, if the truth was told," Dejon said. I remembered thinking the same thing in school last year.

"After the enslaved were finally free, it took years before the Africans on the southern tip would know."

"That's why we celebrate Juneteenth." I said.

"A remembrance holiday, so that you never forget," Mr. Turner added. "The north said that the enslaved were free, unless found guilty of a crime. Guess which areas were created to promote the most crimes? They shipped as many Black people to Africa as they could and left the rest of our people here with almost no resources.

"They made millions for this country and after so called freedom; the only place that the former enslaved could find work was on the same plantations they had left.

119

"Later, the coppers organized a huge coward group called the Ku Klux Klan to kill Africans or force them to kill each other."

"Don't show us any of that," I almost interrupted him.

"I know that your spirit is temporarily broken from what you have learned and witnessed, but trust me, it will rebuild better than before now that you know. I won't show you more of these evil images, but only because you are witnessing one now."

I was relieved.

"Decade after decade the country has tormented the lives of Black people. There was a law that said they could not work in viable areas, but then jailed them for not working. There was a law that said they had to pay taxes, but they couldn't vote for their own leaders. There was a law that said they couldn't take a White man to court although those were the only people stealing from them.

"We then organized groups to combat these problems and the government used coppers to have them poison themselves with drugs that were created in a lab. Poison that most were not even aware of the side effects.

Then after you sold or did the poison, or didn't have a job, guess where you went?"

"Into slavery?" I asked.

"Yes, the penal system which is modern slavery. This is the place where they make your high dollar cell phones and computers."

"So, they kill the Africans in the Congo for the mineral to create those products, and then force the Africans in America to assemble them?" Dejon asked.

"Then excite the Africans who are not in the penal system to buy them," Mr. Turner added.

"I would have never seen it like that. We are screwed all the way around."

"Why do you think I am showing you this?" Nat Turner asked us both.

"So I don't go to work today?" Dejon asked.

"So that we do something about it?" I asked.

"Know Thyself." Mr. Turner disappeared and we were stuck behind that wall, holding an article and the Solar Calendar, still afraid for our lives.

Historical Figures

Queen Nzingha 1583 – 1663
Zumbi 1655 – 1695
Nat Turner 1800 – 1831
Marcus Garvey 1887 – 1940
Patrice Lumumba 1925 – 1961
Malcolm X 1925 – 1965

Map of Location

TO GET THE
LATEST
INFORMATION
ON THE
DEMARCUS JONES
SERIES, RELEASE
DATES AND
CONTESTS,
CONNECT WITH
US ONLINE AT

WWW.DEMARCUSJONES.COM

Made in the USA
San Bernardino, CA
22 March 2017